I0829557

Inspired by Nature

An Anthology of Poetry and Short Stories

by

CONTRIBUTORS

Genevra Adams

John Aaron Adams

Scott Fuller

Gail J. VanWart

Inspired by Nature

An Anthology of Poetry and Short Stories

Published by
Out of the Blue LLC
PO Box 102
Holden, Maine 04429
outofthebluellc.com

ISBN 978-0-9848206-9-6

Library of Congress Control Number
2017903096

© Copyright 2017 Peaked Mountain Farm
and Native Polinator Sanctuary. All Rights Reserved.

*All contributions included in this anthology
are used with permission for one time publishing rights.
Each contributor retains full copyright of their own work.*

Contents

I, *Scott Fuller*..1

II, *Scott Fuller* 2

III, *Scott Fuller* 3

IV, *Scott Fuller*..4

V, *Scott Fuller* 5

VI, *Scott Fuller*..6

VII, *Scott Fuller* 7

VIII, *Scott Fuller* 8

IX, *Scott Fuller*..9

X, *Scott Fuller*...10

XI, *Scott Fuller*..11

XII, *Scott Fuller* 12

Spring Awakening, *Genevra Adams*..13

August in Maine, *Genevra Adams* 13

Smokey Air, *Genevra Adams* 13

The Fox, *Scott Fuller*...14

The Bee, *Scott Fuller*...16

Waiting, *Scott Fuller*...17

Star Shadows, *Scott Fuller* 18

When Young Love Becomes Old, *Scott Fuller*................................19

Secret of the Shells, *Scott Fuller* 20

Whales off Green Island, *Scott Fuller*..22

Popham Beach, *Scott Fuller* 23

Reverie, *Scott Fuller* 24

The Spring, *Scott Fuller* 26

The Shallows, *Scott Fuller* 28

Thinking of You, *Gail J. VanWart* 29

Petals in the Brook, *Scott Fuller* 30

October Rain, *Scott Fuller* 32

John's Poem, *John Aaron Adams* 34

Mildred the Stubborn Maple Leaf, *Gail J. VanWart* 36

Hector, *Scott Fuller* 41

DEDICATION

I would like to dedicate my efforts to this anthology to
Carol Cramer Drummond for her faith and support
over the years. — *Scott Fuller*

I

Scott Fuller

The wind moves across the lake

Rolling up white waves;

The waterfowl are silent.

© Copyright Scott Fuller, April 28, 2012

II
Scott Fuller

The robin hops carefully

Through the rain wet grass

For worms forced to the surface.

© Copyright Scott Fuller, July 22, 2012

III

Scott Fuller

The boat plows through the darkness

Its wake florescent

As the mirrored moon dances.

© Copyright Scott Fuller, July 22, 2012

IV
Scott Fuller

The rain falls gently to earth

Washing all things clean,

Butterflies wait beneath leaves.

© Copyright Scott Fuller, March 7, 2012

V

Scott Fuller

The mayfly paused briefly

Above still water

As, silently, a trout rose.

© Copyright Scott Fuller, April 19, 2012

VI

Scott Fuller

As the sun sets in the sea,

The water is like glass

The shimmering, white moon.

© *Copyright Scott Fuller, April 31, 2012*

VII·

Scott Fuller

As we motor slowly through fog,

Water still as death;

A gray seal floats in the quiet.

© Copyright Scott Fuller, April 9, 2012

VIII

Scott Fuller

Moonlight plays across the lawn,

Peopling the shade

With cold souls of distant stars.

© Copyright Scott Fuller, June 1, 2012

IX

Scott Fuller

Web stretched across a patch

Of green, close mown lawn,

Dew dangling from the silk strands.

© Copyright Scott Fuller, June 1, 2012

X

Scott Fuller

Cold, sparkling clear water falls

On and over hard,

Gray feldspar sprinkled granite.

© Copyright Scott Fuller, May 31, 2012

XI

Scott Fuller

I walk soft on dew wet grass

To a crushed, warm spot;

Deer bound through broad, rolling fields.

© *Copyright Scott Fuller, May 31, 2012*

XII

Scott Fuller

Snow covered apple bough

Hangs over a cliff;

Gray waves roar and pound below.

© Copyright Scott Fuller, March 8, 2012

Spring Awakening
Genevra Adams

hear the crickets sing
daffodils, tulips, snowdrops
Sakura means life

© Copyright Genevra Adams, 2016

August in Maine
Genevra Adams

barefoot on the sand
blueberry pie and campfires
beach roses, salty air

© Copyright Genevra Adams, 2016

Smokey Air
Genevra Adams

crisp air, apple pie
burst of colors red and gold
harvest moon glows orange

© Copyright Genevra Adams, 2016

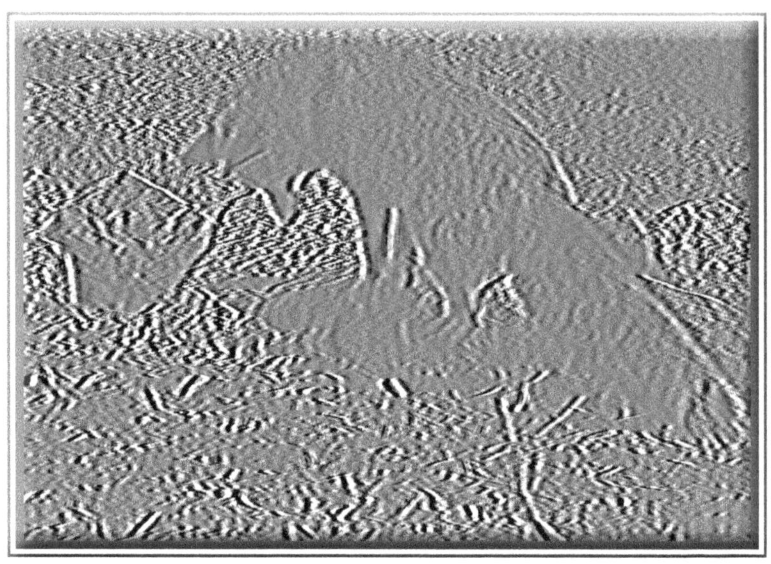

The Fox

Scott Fuller

Mornings, the fox reclined in late spring grass
At the door of an old, ramshackle shed
Not quite hidden from cars as they passed
On the road which by the farmhouse led.

I looked forward, as I drove by each day,
To seeing it resting mid the warming light
Of those flower dazzled fields in May:
A sweet reminder of a gentler life.

Then, early one day on my morning ride,
As by the farm shed I slowly passed,
I saw that the field was newly mown
And all gone was the tall, sheltering grass.

Gone also was the fox from shed and field
And I was sad that the creature was gone,
Displaced for the sake of the farmer's yield,
 So, I imagined, homeless and alone.

Then, some weeks later, farther up the road,
While driving by another working farm,
I spied the fox on skidder scared ground
And I quickly stopped the car in alarm.

This farmer I knew, kept a large flock of Geese
And now my red friend was in great danger,
But it also stopped, and, in naive peace,
Looked back with the cool glance of a stranger.

The eyes betrayed a casual wonder
At my mysterious curiosity,
Then it resumed its loping wander
In its own, compelling, odyssey.

To my displaced friend I bid farewell,
In summer lands may you forever dwell.

© Copyright Scott Fuller, September 21, 2013

The Bee

Scott Fuller

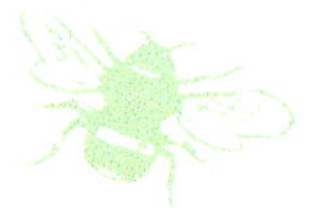

The bee hovers tentatively
Above the blossom
Before landing
And scurrying headlong
Into the trumpet.

Momentarily

It reemerges
Petulant and disheveled,
Pollen,
Lint like,
Clinging randomly
To its fuzzy body.

The bee seems to collect its dignity
And leaps into the
Shimmering air
To continue
Its all important rounds.

© Copyright Scott Fuller, May 16, 2012

Waiting
Scott Fuller

The moon rides high in the summer night,
Reflecting off the cloud tops, muting the stars
And shimmering on the black top of the country road.

I stand on the porch.
Fireflies bounce and dart on the warm breeze
As crickets, peepers and a whippoorwill
Raise a symphony from the shadows.

My eyes strain through the moon glow
Seeking approaching headlights
Where the road disappears in the distant trees.

My ears work to pick through the evening music
For the hum of an automobile engine.

I stand on the porch waiting.

© Copyright Scott Fuller, February 14, 2012

Star Shadows

Scott Fuller

We are two silhouettes
Against the night sky
Foiled by the Milky Way
And to the casual eye
This is all that defines us,

In the silver stained dark
I see a glimmer
In the depth of your eyes.

A promise of the morning
From the warmth
Of your soul.

We speak softly
Through the weight of night
To feel the heat of life
In the whispered words
That brush our dew damp faces.

We are pregnant with the coming day
And though the night
Is wonder beyond telling
Tomorrow comes in a mist

From our trembling lips.

© Copyright Scott Fuller, April, 2015

Sonnet

When Young Love Becomes Old

Scott Fuller

When we were young and green we knew the thrill
Of moon enchanted night and dew damp dawn
On deserted beach and high, wind swept hill
Amid wild flowers and tame summer lawns
We laid us down where fate and passion chose
And did not rise again before the sun
And our fresh love blossomed like the savage rose
When cool winter ends and warm spring's begun.
Those days of innocence are behind us
And the cold world has trailed and tracked us down,
All the evening magic and youth fed lust
Are in worry, dept and dear children drowned
While our once fierce hearts are worn to dust
And in dry respectability bound.

Come my love, fly to me, this one last time
To embrace, on moon lit shore, a love sublime.

© Copyright Scott Fuller, September 28, 2013

Secret of the Shells

Scott Fuller

Shells on the sand know a thing,
 A thing or two about what's true.

 Shells on the salt, wet sand
 Hold the memory
 Of love in murky shade
 Deep under breaking waves.

 Look you to the tumult
 Of salt flesh
 Beneath a milky moon.

 Come you, now
 All creaky with
  Invertebrate lust
 To the deep
 And spiny secrets
 That the shells
 Are memories of.

 Show the way
 That life becomes live
  Before God the sun
 And that devil moon
 As told by the wise old shells.

As we walk along the strand
The sea birds call among themselves
 In the hollow approach of night
And as we look into the deep sky
 I quote Spencer and speak of coming storm
And you pronounce yourself forewarned.

And, as it happens
We two know a little something
About the secret of the shells
But there is more than a fairy child
In a trough between the waves.

I hold a shell to my ear
And is it the sea I hear
Or is it the whispered statement
Of a wordless God?

Is this then, where the secret lies,
In the voice of rising tides?
Was there a thought before there was a mind?

Share a secret with me
Before the rising sea.

© Copyright Scott Fuller, February 2, 2016

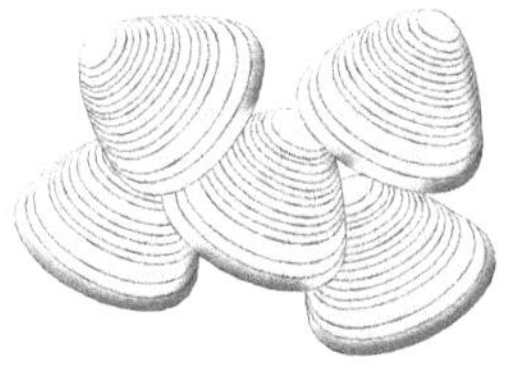

Whales off Green Island

Scott Fuller

Turbulent water, blue, black
Under the thick grey mist
Hide secrets like my mother did.

Small secrets in the white caps
Of milling little creatures
That one day will chuckle your eyes
Wide with the wonder of childhood.

Then, the whales come,
Monstrous in their silence,
Rising, first one and then another
Like the waves they people,
Unexpected, yet looked for,
Hidden in the surf,
A conspiracy of worlds
To make you gasp
In awe and surprise.

Secret things that stride the wet earth
In the cloak of storm clouds.

And you?

You might be innocence itself
As you stand delighted and deceived
Within a life that never was.

© Copyright Scott Fuller

Popham Beach

Scott Fuller

Night rolls in on Popham Beach
Like mist off the sea.
I am sprawled before a large
Popplestone fireplace
In a beach house
Sprung straight from the shore.

Driftwood piled high
In graceful curves and soft grays
On either side of the fireplace

Art of the sea.

Sculpture turns painting
As tongues of flame
Lick away the gentle forms,
Transforming them into
Dancing wisps of watercolor.

I am alone with my thoughts
In the pulsing light
While outside, on the April evening shore
The barren waves
Whispers menacingly through the timbers.

I am the only living
Thing in the Universe tonight
And as I step out under the stars
I am cloaked in a wonderful terror
That wraps me in the evening cold.

© Copyright Scott Fuller

Reverie

Scott Fuller

The full Moon mounts to the zenith
In the August Heaven
As I move easily
Along the wooded path
Skirting the still, forest pond.

I shelter in the pale, glowing air
And the Moon shade of the leafy trees
As, somewhere in the distance,
A loon calls and, a moment later,
 A fox replies.

I have no company
But I am not alone.

It feels as though all
Is contained
Within my soul.

I am the loon
Calling among the stars,

I am the fox
Waiting patiently
In the golden grass,

I am the very light
Born of the Sun kissed Moon
Shimmering in the defuse mist
Gathering over motionless water.
I am so at one
With the evening

I might

Almost,

Be resting in your arms.

© Copyright Scott Fuller, July 23, 2016

The Spring

Scott Fuller

I came to the spring

Where it
bubbled up
Clear and cool
Under the shade
Of beech trees,

Thirsty
On a warm day in June.

A few
Ancient brown leaves
Lay
Slowly, softly disintegrating
Into the delicate,
Dark lace of the bottom,
Framed in a rim of moss.

A blue porcelain dipper
Hung, inviting, from
An old, forked stick
Stuck deep into the stony,
Mossy ground.

Taking the dipper
From were it hung,

I knelt
To scoop the
Nearly invisible water
From the pool.

The taste was \sweet
As home
After a long trip,

Refreshing body
And soul together.

The coolness
Ran through my body
Like a shudder of pleasure

And I was replete.

Again I scooped
Water from the spring
And this dipper full
I poured over
My head
As a self baptism.

The perfectly clear,
Perfectly cold
Water

Ran over
My burning flesh
Like cleansing fire.

It was a gift of stone
And storm
And Winter snows

Given secretly
And sweetly
In the shade
Of the beeches.

Overhead
The new leaves
Moved

As though
The sky

Had breathed a sigh.

© *Copyright Scott Fuller, November 14, 2016*

The Shallows

Scott Fuller

The fry of various fish species
In their separate schools
Dart about in the small, shallow cove
Like a rainbow in a quiet tornado.

They gather in this shelter
Against the deep, open water
And the terrors that lie
Hiding in the vast darkness.

Here, under the pines
Seeming to play below
The noon day sun,
Flash denizens of tomorrows depths.

As, just beyond the reef
The ancient monsters
Wait, as they have always waited
To welcome the intrepid.

© Copyright Scott Fuller, October 17, 2016

Thinking of You
Gail J. VanWart

Petals from my roses
wither on the floor.
Silhouettes of good night kisses
no longer shade my door.

I decline from singing
melodious tunes on summer days.
Stars refuse my wishes
and the moon is recluse in haze.

Once priceless treasures
carried within my heart,
now merely tarnished memories
as I think of you.

© *Copyright Gail J. VanWart, 2017*

Petals in the Brook
Scott Fuller

I hiked the gap between two mountains
On a sunny morning in mid-spring,
As the cool dawn air, alive with bird song,
Rode the rising, swirling, silver mists.

I chanced upon a brook meandering
Quietly down the gentle slope
Under the birches and the stunted pines
Protected from the heat of the sun.

Here, in the cool, moving waters,
Little green trout lurked, vigilant.

Under the brown tinted foam,
Spinning lazily at the bottom
Of tiny falls and over eddies
Waiting for less vigilant prey.

When I closed my eyes for a moment,
The moving, falling, water seemed
To ring like chimes across the slope
And through the whispering birches.

To my weary mind, the soft voices
Of this ancient, unspoiled place
Beckoned my worldly heart and soul
To a place sacred beyond thought.

I was certain that forgotten gods
Lingered here between the walls
Which rose steeply and solemnly
Over this sweet and secret Heaven.

I seemed to stand in a pagan temple
Though I did not feel inclined to bow
But to throw my head back in exaltation
And to sing in union with the wind.

I was home from the world
Built of my own, manufactured
Monsters and self conjured nightmares
Back to the blessed cradle of beginning.

From somewhere in these mountains
The source of all life, sacred and profane
Burst through the broken stones
To nurse and baptize the hungry and lost.

When, finally, I came through the pass
My tired body, drenched in sweat
And aching with much exertion,
Felt yet fulfilled and renewed.

In my mind, I brought away
The secrets of that holy place
And the cool waters of those hills
Feed and refresh my reborn heart.

© Copyright Scott Fuller, July 27, 2016

October Rain
For Darlene
Scott Fuller

The leaves of October
Cover the Ground
Like a Brilliant
Paper carpet.

The carpet,
Yellow, red and brown,
Is slick with falling rain
As the grim sky
Writes a poem
Of time and
Happenstance
On glossy
Stationery.

A smell, sweet as death
Rises like a ghost,
Not Quite invisible,
Dancing just above
The cold,
Damp
Ground.

Memories resurrect
Sad and lovely
As this dying season.

Hazy now,
But we children,
Playing like a
Happy song
On an old victrola
Under the veranda
While the dairy cows
On the hill above us
Ignored our secrets.

I hear your name
In this poem of autumn
Speaking on the
Chilly wind,

And your hair
Had the scent of
Rain and leaves

And the melody
Among the branches
Is the music of children
In a conspiracy of make believe.

I walk in a forest of ghosts
Under the sweetest rain.

© Copyright Scott Fuller, November 12, 2016

John's Poem
Traditions Last Forever
John Aaron Adams

Running,
running,
going through the field,
trying not to ruin the blueberries.

My mother catching up.
As we run, I think,
let's pick some blueberries.
This is the annual thing we do every year.

The years go by
and I think to myself;
when I have kids
I will do the same thing.

Running,
running,
going through the field,
trying not to ruin the blueberries.

My son and I
doing the same thing
that my mother and I did
when I was young.

All of us get bowls full of berries;
bring them back to Gram's house
to make something out of it.
This is tradition that will last forever!

Running,
running,
my son and his kids
trying not to ruin the blueberries,
going through the field
to get bowls of blueberries.

© Copyright John Aaron Adams, 2005

Mildred the Stubborn Maple Leaf

Gail J. VanWart

Mildred was born early one spring at the tip of the topmost branch of a tall and majestic maple tree. It was long before all the snow had melted in the woods, but mother maple tree had Mildred wrapped so snugly in her protective covering she didn't notice the lingering chill of winter at all.

As the weather grew warmer, Mildred grew bigger and stronger. She stretched and pushed at her covering and, little by little, nudged it away until she could peek out into the wondrous world.

When Mildred saw the big blue sky with its fluffy clouds and sparkling rays of sunshine, she was delighted.

"I must see more!" She grunted as she pushed and pushed with greater determination to shed more of her covering.

The spring days bathed Mildred with rain showers then dried her with gentle breezes as she worked. Then it happened. As Mildred stretched to greet the sun one morning, her covering popped right off her back and floated slowly to the forest floor. Mildred was standing alone on her very own stem!

Trembling with excitement she uncurled herself.

"Hooray!" she shouted as she stretched. "I'm a real leaf!"

All summer long Mildred frolicked on her treetop. She played tag with the wind, and danced in the rain. When she wasn't playing games, she pretended to be queen of the entire woodland. Overlooking the forest from her treetop throne, Mildred thought she knew everything there was to know about the world.

Who else could know all the other kinds of trees and recognize each bird by its songs? Who, but she, could describe the laughable antics of the chipmunks and the squirrels. Why she could show you the zigzagging trail of the rabbit and winding path of the deer, and point out the hiding places of the raccoon, the skunk, and the bobcat. She even knew all the secrets of the sly fox and where lady's slippers and violets grow.

One day, late in the summer, Mildred looked at the world below her treetop throne and exclaimed, "Life is grand at the top of my tree!"

"That may be so," responded the leaf below her, "but it will soon be time to leave this tree and prepare for winter. Our color is already changing."

"Leave this tree? You must be kidding!" Mildred was shocked at the mere thought of it. She'd been so busy playing and pretending she hadn't noticed the changes taking place around her or the bright red she was turning.

"When it is time, we will leave the tree," stated the leaf below her. "It has been decided for us by life, itself. The autumn wind will blow us from our branches. Then we can go to the forest floor to serve the earth."

"I don't believe it," Mildred said. She was sure this would not happen to her and made up her mind to pay no attention to the other leaf.

Soon, the days started growing shorter and the wind became much sharper. The rain was no longer warm enough to dance in and Mildred tried to shake off its chill. She had watched lots of birds fly far, far away into the sky and seen the chipmunks and squirrels gathering nuts and seeds endlessly each day. The entire forest burst into glorious shades of yellow and red all around her, but even so, Mildred still did not believe she would ever leave her tree.

One morning autumn's frost arrived to paint beautiful white, icy, designs throughout the woods.

"Ouch! That stings! Get off me!" shouted Mildred at the frost.

"Don't be such a cry baby," sneered the leaf below her. "We'll be falling to the ground soon where we'll be much warmer."

"You can fall to the ground if you want to," responded Mildred, "but I will never leave this tree."

Then came the coldest night Mildred had ever experienced. A harsh wind that blew fearlessly through the woods shook the trees with all its might. Dry leaves filled the air as it whipped them from their branches with its mighty gusts.

"Good-bye Mildred," called out the leaf below her as it sprang to the air and twirled down, down, down to the forest floor. Mildred held on with all her might. She was not giving up her tree for any amount of wind!

She was extremely tired when morning came, she had not slept at all. The sun chased the wind away, but its rays weren't strong enough to warm her now. Looking around her, Mildred could see only a few other leaves who remained on their trees. As she watched, some of them rustled crisply and leaped willfully into the air to join the others on the ground. The forest floor was now blanketed with beautiful autumn leaves. But Mildred still did not want to join them.

"What good are leaves on the forest floor?" she asked. "How foolish to let the trees stand barren and cold."

In time, Mildred was the only leaf left clinging to a tree in the entire forest. It was bitterly cold and she'd become quite brittle. She found it difficult to wrap herself around her branch for support.

"Why can't I stay green and soft like you?" she asked a needle on a nearby pine tree.

"Because your job is done in the tree top," the pine needle replied. "You should move to the ground to continue your life there. When winter comes, my job is to protect the birds and animals who remain in the forest all year. After the summer, your job is to protect and nourish the flowers that will grow next spring. You should join your friends before the big storms come."

Mildred looked at the lifeless piles of leaves her friends had become. They were all rusty brown and wrinkled. It didn't appear as if they were doing much of anything at all. "No. I'll help you protect the wildlife instead," she replied.

"Ha! What can one little leaf like you protect up here this time of year?" laughed the pine needle. "You can hardly protect yourself."

Mildred still clung to her branch. She'd heard that spring followed winter. Spring will surely make me soft and green again, she thought. She dreamed of dancing in the rain and playing in the sun as the days and nights grew colder—and colder.

Winter had begun. The sky darkened and the air filled with feathery snowflakes. Mildred rolled herself around her branch as best she could. She'd frozen in the most awkward position and could hardly move.

She watched as the leaves on the ground snuggled deeper and deeper under the fluffy snow until she could no longer see them.

"Look at you," said the pine needle one day. "You have been frozen stiff for months while your friends are all safe and warm under the snow."

Indeed Mildred was frozen so solidly she couldn't answer. All she could do was cling to her tree and hope spring would soon arrive.

It took longer than she had anticipated, but spring eventually crept into the woods and chased winter's wind and snow away. Mildred finally thawed, but was so crisp she cracked when she tried to unfold herself. No matter, she thought, spring will soon fix me.

Little did she know, at that very moment, a tiny bump on her branch was growing into a bud right under her stem.

As the days grew warmer, the bud began to push at its covering, just like Mildred had done the year before.

"Hey! Who are you? Why are you pushing at my stem?" Mildred was startled by the bud's presence.

"I'm just Mary, the maple bud. I'm sorry if I pushed you, but you have to move so I can become a leaf," responded the bump under her stem.

Mildred remembered how hard she had worked to become a leaf. "Okay. But please try pushing in another direction so my stem isn't bothered," she instructed. She was lonely for company and actually welcomed the thought of another leaf to talk to.

"I'll try," agreed Mary as she pushed and nudged away from Mildred as much as possible. But it wasn't long before there was no more room for Mary to grow inside her covering and off it popped. Mary suddenly uncurled as a new leaf and swept Mildred right off the branch.

Down, down, down she floated until she gently landed on some soft damp moss. Mildred was shocked. How could that new little leaf sweep her from her branch so easily, after all she had been through?

As Mildred looked around the forest floor she became frightened. She could not see her friends who had fallen there last autumn. She felt lost and alone. "Where is everybody?" she cried.

"Here, under the new buds of the violets," called back one leaf.

"Over here, around the roots of the fiddleheads," shouted another.

"We're all here," stated the leaf that used to be on the branch below her. "We're all part of the earth now. We feed the soil with our goodness to make things grow. Too bad you don't want to help. It's an important job."

Mildred looked up at her tree. Its branches were full of new soft green leaves and the birds were returning to build their nests. She looked at herself. She was brown, brittle, all out of shape and full of holes. Then for the first time, Mildred understood the full meaning of life. Her friends had become part of the very heart of the world.

"Oh," she moaned, "if only I hadn't been so stubborn. Now there is no place for me and nothing for me to do." Mildred felt ashamed and useless.

"It is never too late to change your ways," whispered a sweet comforting voice.

"Who are you? And where are you?" Mildred could not see the owner of the voice anywhere.

"Why Mildred, I am everywhere," replied Mother Nature. "Now if you will really stop being stubborn, I can make you happy and useful again."

"I will never be stubborn again," Mildred promised. "How can I be happy?"

"It's easy Mildred. Just let yourself be what you are and don't try to be something you aren't," replied Mother Nature.

Mildred settled into the moss as she thought about the advise. It felt really good to rest there after the long hard winter. In fact, it felt so good she drifted off to sleep.

When Mildred awoke, she discovered the most wonderful thing had happened during her nap. The beautiful blossom of a pink Lady Slipper bobbed gently in the breeze above her. Its leaves had sprouted right through one of Mildred's holes. She was keeping the soil around its roots moist and nutritious. It was such an easy job she hadn't even realized she had been doing it.

Mildred was soft again. She wasn't green, like back in the days when she lived in the tree, but she was now the caretaker of new green things that would grow year after year. She was the softness of the earth and part of life's miracle.

© Copyright Gail J. VanWart, 1989

Hector

Scott Fuller

In nineteen eighty in the tiny village of Combs Pond, Maine, I had, though I was still in college, just married. My wife, Wanda, and I were spending Halloween with her family. Combs is situated on a strip of land running between Combs Pond and Gray Lake. There was a summer population of perhaps a thousand, made up mostly of camp owners from the surrounding small cities and a year round population of less than two hundred souls. The town had a three room school house that also served the neighboring town of Kentston.

The center of Combs business and social life is the Combs General Store, which, in nineteen eighty, was owned and operated by Bill Clayton and his wife, Naomi. At the store you could get most of your basic needs met at an inflated price as Bill, a couple of times a week, would drive to one of the "cities" and load his pick-up with what ever was on sale at the supermarkets and come back with the haul. There were grocery staples, common hardware items, gasoline, diesel fuel, kerosene, propane and even sporting goods including fishing tackle and ammunition. There was, near the checkout counter, a large bulletin board on which to post messages to the community. The store was a favorite
hangout for locals, a place where gossip and ideas were exchanged.

The store has changed hands many times in its history but, by now, it had been owned by the Claytons for several years. Bill was from Portsmouth, New Hampshire. His family, however, had owned a camp on

Combs Pond for several generations so Bill and his wife fit right and in fact, had established a town tradition of their own. There was a rumor that Bill had someone named Hector living in the cellar of Combs General Store.

I first became acquainted with this "legend" while watching Freddy, my six year old brother-in-law Prepare for Halloween. I was sitting in an armchair in the living room studying for a French exam when I was distracted by a conversation between Freddy and his mother, Doreen. Freddy's face was white with make-up and his hair had been stained black and swept straight back. He had a natural widow's peak that worked well with the Dracula motif. He already wore the fangs and cape and Doreen was applying red color to his lips and creating droplets of "blood" to one corner of his mouth. They were having an intense discussion regarding someone named Hector who, from eavesdropping, I learned lived chained in the cellar of Bill's store. When I interrupted to ask Freddy who Hector was, he told me that Hector was a monster belonging to Bill Clayton.

"Have you ever met Hector" I asked Freddy.

"Yes I have, last year," Freddy replied.

"What does Hector look like?" I continued.

"He's big and green and has long sharp teeth" Freddy said, his eyes wide with fear.

I asked Doreen to explain what Freddy meant but she just turned away from me and refused to discuss it.

I have never been intimately involved with a village as small as Combs but I have heard that strange, sometimes terrible things went on in these little, isolated communities and that the locals always conspired to protect each others secrets from the outside world. I suspected that I had just stumbled upon just such a secret; Bill Clayton might keeping a mentally, and possibly physically, disabled relative or ward locked in his cellar. I went looking for Wanda to get a better understanding of who Hector was and what his situation was. After all, Bill was a family friend and Combs was her hometown. Presumably she would be privy to its dark underbelly. I could almost hear banjos.

When I asked her who Hector was, all I got from Wanda was a cryptic glare.

"What goes on in the Clayton family is nobodies business." she said gravely.

"If Bill is keeping a disabled relative chained in his cellar then it's everyone's business, including the Department of Human Services. In a more civilized community, people wouldn't sit still for an animal being treated this way." I argued. "What is it teaching Freddy about the value and dignity of human life if he sees his role models treating others this way?

And how can this situation be so casual that small children know about it and discuss it openly?"

"Oh, Freddy knows about it because on Halloween night, Bill lets the kids go down to the cellar to see him. It's a big deal with them." Wanda said.

I stared at her blankly. This was insane. This couldn't be happening., I needed to see for myself.

My curiosity piqued, I drove out to the store to observe the situation first hand.

It was late afternoon and Bill was standing near the door at the center of a group of children as they overwhelmed him with questions about Hector. Was Hector still living in the cellar? Was Bill going to let them see him this year. Were Hector's chains strong enough to hold him? Had he been fed recently? Bill stood there grinning though out while giving vague, ambiguous replies.

I started questioning the children. Had they ever actually seen Hector? Everyone of them insisted that they had. What did Hector look like? Every witness gave a different description. No two accounts were even similar. When I cornered Bill and asked him about Hector, to my indignation, he winked and smiled.

Later, when a group of trick or treaters gathered outside at the cellar bulkhead behind the store, Bill disappeared down the inside cellar steps. A friend of Bill's opened the bulkhead to let the kids go down. They barely got to the bottom step when the chains began clanking and a long, low moan reverberated through the dark cellar. The children screamed and fell over each other getting up the stairs. When they got their breaths, I again questioned each child and again I got a variety of descriptions.

At that moment, realizing that the cellar door had been left ajar and no one was around, I seized the opportunity to sneak into the cellar. The shadows made no sound. The cellar was empty. I went back into the store and there was Bill, grinning, looking no different than he did every day.

That's when I realized that the true mystery behind Hector was that he had never really been seen by anyone. It was obvious from my conversations with the youngsters that they were all absolutely sure that they had seen him. They had seen a shadow and heard a moan and their vital imaginations had filled in the blanks, That's how the mind works.

Although Hector was a phantom who lived in the shadows of imagination, his image was corporal and vivid enough to any child brave enough to challenge Comb's dark secret.

© *Copyright Scott Fuller, October 12, 2004*

This anthology was compiled by a small group of creative people,
gently guided by Scott Fuller, who gathered during the summer of 2016
in Dedham, Maine on Peaked Mountain Farm and Native Pollinator Sanctuary.
They explored how the principles of composition influenced their writing
and its relationship to inspiration gained from nature.

Back Cover Photograph by Gail J. VanWart

www.ingramcontent.com/pod-product-compliance
Lightning Source LLC
Chambersburg PA
CBHW051115300726
48981CB00002B/139

9780984820696